IN A DEAF PERSON'S HOME, LIGHTS FLASH AS A DOORBELL.

THIS BOOK IS DEDICATED TO ALL THE DEAF CHILDREN OF THE WORLD.

THANKS TO THOSE WHO APPEAR IN THIS BOOK: SETH BRAVIN, STACY NOWAK, MARTIN STERNBERG, LYNNETTE TAYLOR, JONATHAN TURNER AND FANNY YEH; AND TO THOSE WHO HELPED: PAULA BENTON, PHIL BRAVIN, MARY ANN KLEIN, DEBORAH MATTHEWS, BOB MATTHEWS, CATHY MARKLAND, MARCIA NOWAK, JANICE RIMLER, JAMES K. ROSS, VALERIE ROSS, AND DAVID AND JO ANN WEINRIB.

HANDTALK BIRTHDAY

A NUMBER & STORY BOOK IN SIGN LANGUAGE

REMY CHARLIP   MARY BETH   GEORGE ANCONA

FOUR WINDS PRESS   NEW YORK   NEW YORK

THE TEXT OF THIS BOOK IS SET IN CENTURY EXPANDED. THE PHOTOGRAPHS WERE TAKEN WITH 120 EKTACHROME TRANSPARENCY FILM AND TUNGSTEN LIGHTING, AND ARE REPRODUCED IN FULL COLOR.

LIBRARY OF CONGRESS CATALOGING-IN-PUBLICATION DATA • CHARLIP, REMY. HANDTALK BIRTHDAY. SUMMARY: WORDS AND SIGN LANGUAGE DEPICT FRIENDS HELPING A DEAF GIRL CELEBRATE HER BIRTHDAY. [1. DEAF—FICTION. 2. BIRTHDAYS—FICTION. 3. SIGN LANGUAGE] I. MARY BETH. II. ANCONA, GEORGE. III. TITLE. PZ7.C3812HAN 1987 [E] 86-22755 ISBN 0-02-718080-8

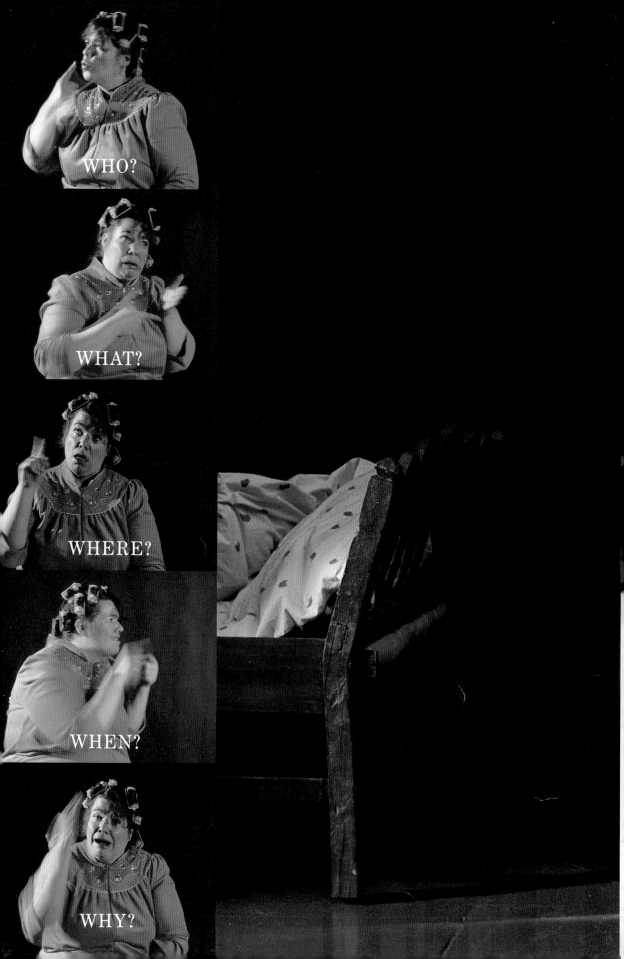

WHAT'S INSIDE?

DRUM?

NO.

NO.

A BIG

N

A

FISH?

NO!

TELL

ME.

OPEN IT!

A HAT!

THANK YOU.

A BASEBALL BAT?

A HOT DOG?

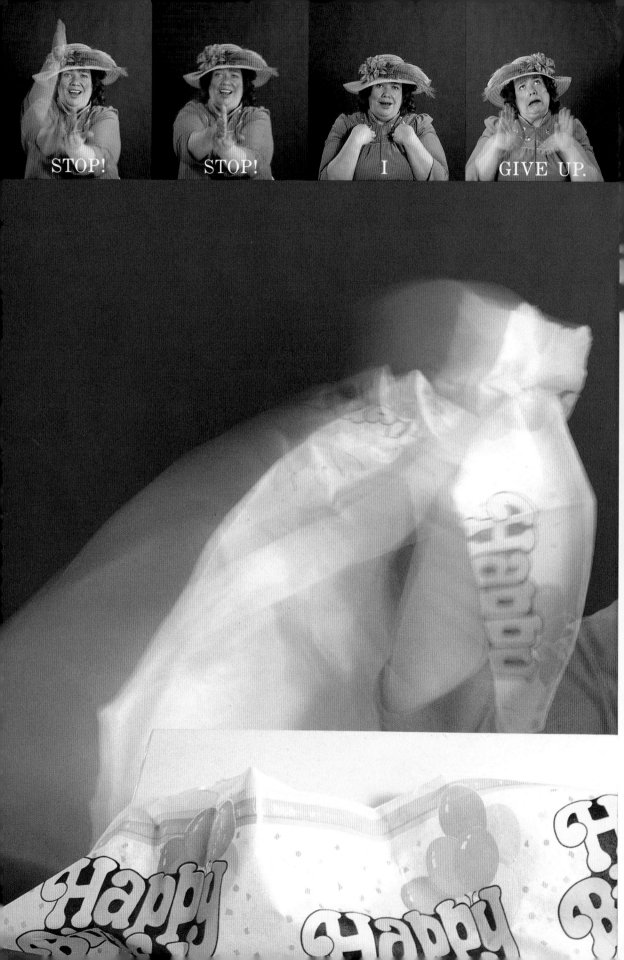

STOP! STOP! I GIVE UP.

YOU'RE DRIVING ME CRAZY.

A FEATHER BOA, AND

IT   MATCHES   MY   HAT!

MORE?

HAPPY BIRTHDAY

HAPPY BIRTHDAY • HAPPY BIRTHDAY • HAPPY

ICE CREAM

BUBBLE GUM

CANDY

TO · YOU

TO · YOU

DEAR · M A R Y B E T H

TO · YOU.

I WISH I COULD

FLY!

CAREFUL.

COME DOWN.

YOU'RE TOO OLD

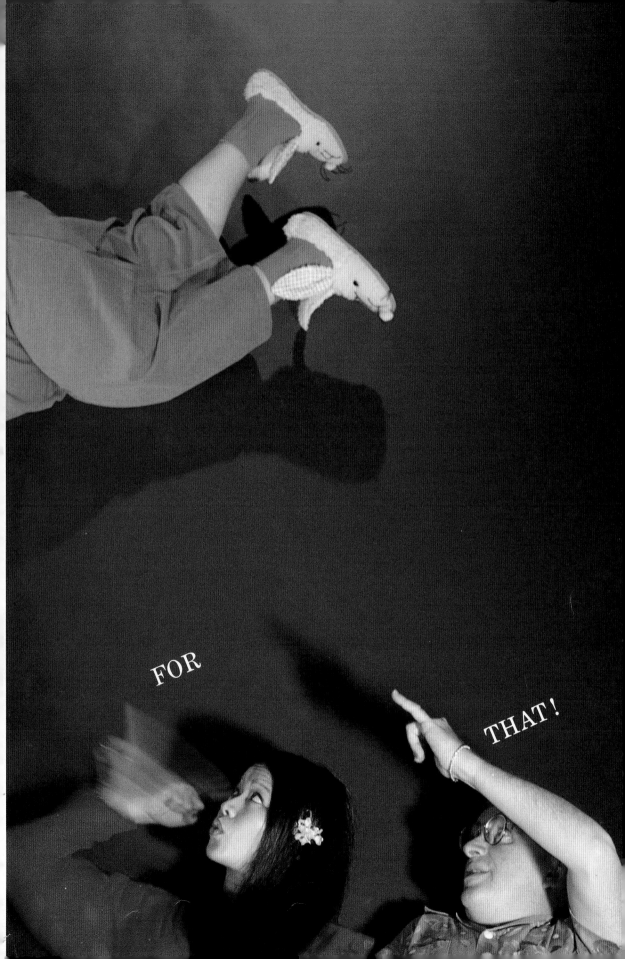

FOR

THAT!

DO YOU

HOW OLD

THINK

I AM?

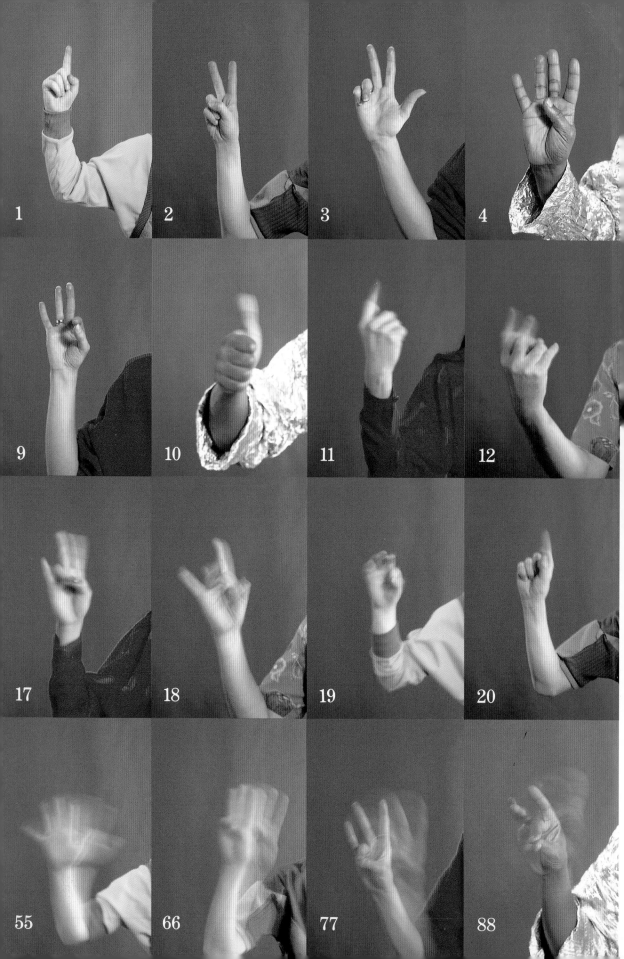

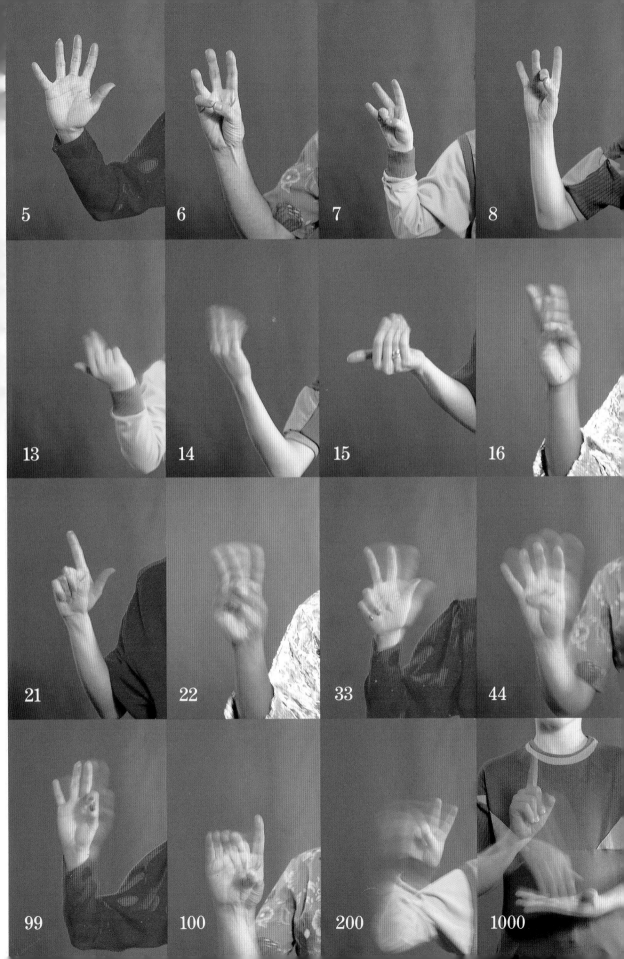

MY SECRET!

43

3